A STORY ABOUT THE . . .

Great Plague

"JENNET'S TALE"
BY HERBIE BRENNAN

A STORY ABOUT THE . . .

Great Plague

"JENNET'S TALE"
BY HERBIE BRENNAN

mammoth

Published in Great Britain 2000 by Mammoth,
an imprint of Egmont Children's Books Limited,
a division of Egmont Holding Limited,
239 Kensington High Street, London W8 6SA.

ISBN 0 7497 3955 X

A CIP catalogue record for this title is available
from the British Library.

Printed and bound in Great Britain.

Contents

The
Fourteenth
Century

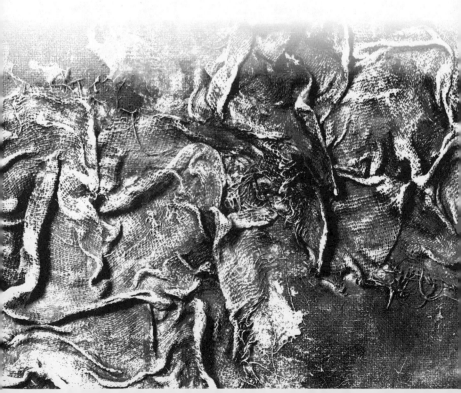

Historians classify the fourteenth century as the High Middle Ages and claim it represented a real improvement on the Dark Ages that went before.

But that's just an improvement by contrast. If you compare it with your life today, the fourteenth century was a foul time to live. It started and finished with English kings whose reigns ended in abysmal failure. And even the long reign of Edward III in the middle of the period brought misery to the people despite his popularity.

The problem, as always, was war. France and England went to war in 1337 and simply wouldn't stop. They stayed at war for so long that the conflict was called the Hundred Years War. But the name doesn't really do it justice. The whole miserable catalogue of bloodshed, greed, aggression and death dragged on until 1453 – fully one hundred and sixteen years.

War was big trouble. It wormed its way into everything. A popular wind instrument of the time was named a 'bombard' after a piece of artillery. The king levied taxes to pay for his military campaigns, and taxes meant hunger and shortages of every kind.

But that was not the worst of it. The Middle Ages began with a plague in AD 542. They drew to a close with another in 1348.

The last plague was much more vicious than the first. It killed and killed and killed, until nearly a third of the total population of Europe disappeared. It triggered famine because there was no one left to till the fields. It changed the face of every country it visited. It haunted human imagination for centuries.

At the time people thought of it as the 'blue sickness'. Today, we call it the Black Death.

Jennet's Tale

1

April 3, 1348

The farm boy, Will Fletcher, broke his leg. I saw them carry him in while I was emptying the chamber pots. There was lots of blood and a sharp piece of white bone poking through his breeches. He was making little mewing noises like a kitten. I never heard a man make noises like that before, nor a boy even.

Goodie Swift sent for Mr Hacket the bone-setter and he came up from the village an hour since. They had Will laid out on the big table in the kitchens. I was put to scrubbing pans so I got to see.

He was just lying there, Will was, as if he was asleep, but his eyes were a little open and he didn't breathe as if he was asleep. Mr Hacket didn't say anything to Will, and Will didn't say anything to Mr Hacket. But Goodie Swift said, 'You take care to do the job right, Hacket. He's a good worker and the Master wouldn't care to lose the use of him.' Mr Hacket tugged his nose and still said nothing.

They cut away the leg of Will's breeches. Goodie Swift complained about the waste of good cloth, although what Will wore was no better than the rest of us. Then they found they couldn't get his boot off because the foot was swollen and they had to cut that away too, so Goodie Swift complained some more. Will never stirred through the whole of it, just lay there breathing like a winded horse.

I never saw a man's leg before, not without his breeches on. The bottom part was white and hairy, but up higher it was blue-black, except for that bit of white bone poking through. All the blood had turned brown and caked like mud, but Mr Hacket didn't seem to take no mind. 'Need two strong men to hold him,' he told Goodie Swift.

While Goodie Swift sent for the strong men, Mr Hacket went out to cut himself a stick. When he came back, he started tearing strips from the leg they took off Will's breeches. 'Waste not, want not,' says he.

They were two big stable boys and I didn't know their names because I'm not allowed near the stables. Mr Hacket told them to hold Will by the shoulders and not to let him move at all. Then he took hold of Will's foot, the one on the end of the broken leg.

Mr Hacket is a short man, near bald and very broad with great big hands. I couldn't stop looking at those hands while he did it. Of a sudden, while the stable boys were holding Will, he jerked back with all his weight on Will's leg and twisted it at the one time. Will gave a bellow like a bull, but the stable boys held him and when I looked, that white bone wasn't sticking through the skin any more. There was just an ooze of fresh blood where it had been.

'Much as I can do,' said Mr Hacket, handing Goodie Swift the stick and the strips he tore from Will's trouser-leg. 'You can put on the splint. Woman's always better at binding than a man – as God made them.'

Goodie Swift doesn't like being told what to do by anybody, least of all a man from the village, so she turned on me. 'What are you gawping at, Jennet? Get back to your work this minute, stupid girl!'

2

April 4, 1348

Father Peter is coming today. That means nobody will beat me.

Today is Sunday, which is the Lord's Day. Father Peter told me God made the whole world in six days and rested on Sunday, which is why nobody should work on Sundays except servants.

Servants have to work on Sundays just like any other day because God made them servants, same as He gave me a hare-lip so my mouth hangs all deformed and twisted my back about so I drag one foot. But I'd have been a servant anyway, so it doesn't matter.

I work harder on Sunday than on any other day. All us servants do, even Goodie Swift who can usually get somebody else to do the work for her. This is because the Master and the Mistress see important people on Sunday and before that hear Mass in their chapel, which is why Father Peter is coming.

I love Father Peter. I would marry him when I grow up were he not a priest. (If he would have a wife with a hare-lip who drags her foot.)

It was Father Peter who taught me how to write. He showed me the secret marks and something in me knew them near right away, even though everybody says I am stupid. And when I didn't know them I worked hard to learn them, and learn them I did. So now I can record my thoughts, which even the Mistress herself cannot do, although I think the Master can sign his name. And I can read the written thoughts of others in some of Father Peter's books.

Father Peter told me to tell none of my learning, for fear they would think I seek to rise above my station which, truly, I do not. He has not spoken this, but I believe he also fears that people might think ill of him for taking an interest in a young girl, even one as ugly as poor Jennet. So my writing is a secret and I guard it carefully.

On a weekday I rise with the light as do all those of the house save our Master and Mistress, but on Sunday I rise with a candle and dress and go to join the others in the kitchens where Goodwife Swift quickly sends us about our business.

It is cleaning mainly. Not our own quarters which are never cleaned, nor the kitchens, which are not seen, but there's fresh rushes to be spread on the floor of the hall where the Master and Mistress sit to eat, and fresh candles to be placed in the chapel, and fresh linen for a bed if a noble stays, and fresh this and fresh that, as well as all the things I usually do like feeding the hens and collecting the eggs and emptying the chamber pots and collecting the kindling and scrubbing the pans and throwing out the slops.

(And on top of this I have Bright Eyes to look after. Bright Eyes is a squirrel I found injured by a fox. I took him in and fed him and now he is better, I cannot get him to leave me. He sleeps and hides in a hole in the wall and comes out when he hears me.)

Goodie Swift set me to do the chapel candles this day. Simple work for a simple girl, says Goodie Swift. But if I linger long enough (and risk a beating on the morrow) I shall see Father Peter, which is worth all.

A pie-man once told me not all great houses have a chapel and Father Peter says this is true, so I am lucky to see such a place. It is truly God's house, for there is coloured glass in the windows, not like the village church which has no windows at all and is damp and dank and dark, more like the Devil's house than God's.

If only I could hear Father Peter say Mass in such a chapel, how soon would my sins be washed away! But the servants, Goodie Swift and all, hear Mass in the great barn and one Sunday a month shivering in the village church, which is not so warm as the barn. Still, I am lucky, am I not, that I may see such a chapel at all? And I am lucky to be friends with a priest like Father Peter. He has told me I am loved by God who does not see my lip or my back or my dragging foot.

So it was that as the first light crept into the sky I entered the chapel with my sack of candles. My stomach was empty of food (for none breaks their fast before the early morning work is done) but filled with the excitement of seeing Father Peter. For on mornings when I am sent with the candles to the chapel, he will sometimes allow me to see the Holy Book itself. While I do not have the Latin to read from it, he will often read to me, showing me with his finger the old Roman words, and telling me what they mean.

I began replacing the old burned-away candles, working as slowly as I dared, and soon after I heard a sound beyond the door and knew it was Father Peter. Of a Sunday, Father Peter sets off in darkness, allowing his horse to find its way, so that he arrives at the Great House by first light. As he had done now.

So I left my sack to one side and hurried to the door to greet him, fast as I could with my stupid dragging foot. And the door opened and a cleric entered.

But it was not Father Peter.

3

April 4, 1348

He was short as Father Peter was tall. He was fat as Father Peter was thin. He was dark as Father Peter was fair. He was ugly as Father Peter was handsome. His eyes were blue and cold.

'What are you doing here, girl?'

I was afraid and so stood looking at him in his black garb like a crow. Gawping, Goodie Swift would say. In my fear I could not speak, not one word.

My silence angered him so that he stepped forward a

pace and cuffed my ear. My head rang. 'Answer me!' he demanded and struck me again, harder this time.

Father Peter said I was not to be beaten on a Sunday. I shuffled away from him, head down, not meeting his eye. 'Candles,' I mumbled.

'Speak up! Speak up!' He had a pretty voice, yet it frightened me more.

'I come to change the candles, sir,' I said, not much louder but a little.

'And see what you can steal?' he sneered. 'See what you can steal from God's house and your Master?'

'No, sir, on my life, sir!' None had ever before accused me of thieving, although there was much of it went on. Perchance they thought me too stupid for theft.

'It will be your life if I catch you!' warned this man. He looked around the chapel and there was greed in his eyes. 'Well, go on!'

'Sir?' I asked, not knowing what he wanted of me.

He made a motion with his hands, like one chasing chickens. 'Change the candles if that was what you were doing.'

'They are changed, sir.'

'Then why are you waiting, you stupid girl? Have you nothing better to do?'

'No, sir. Yes, sir.' I scurried to collect my sack, then scuttled for the door. My head had ceased to ring, but my ear was warm and sore where he had cuffed me. I walked around him to get to the door, keeping as much distance as possible. He smiled at that a little, as if it pleased him to cause fear.

Once past, I unlatched the door and held it so that I might open it quickly and run if he came to hit me again. But I did not pass through the door for my fear of him was overcome by something else. 'Sir,' I said, 'please, sir...'

He had begun to walk towards the altar, my presence

already forgotten, his head high and proud like a great lord who has come to claim his own. Now he turned and glared at me. 'What? What is it?'

'Sir, please, sir, where is Father Peter, sir?'

My question angered him more than any, for his colour rose. I had thought his eyes cold before, but now they were bitter ice. For a moment I thought he would come to strike me again and prepared to run, although in truth I cannot run fast. Even the old hens I feed can outpace me when they have a mind to.

But he did not strike me again, did not so much as move towards me. 'What business is that of yours, girl?' he asked me softly, and his voice hissed like a snake.

I looked away quickly and said nothing. I stood clinging to the door, staring down at my feet.

In a moment, strangely, the anger seemed to drain out of him. As the silence stretched, I risked glancing at him, but moving my eyes only, not my head. There was an expression on his face I could not understand, not anger, not concern, but a sort of wary pleasure. When he spoke, it was as if he spoke to himself, not to me.

'Father Peter,' he said, 'has failed to report for his duties these past two days. Father Peter –' For a moment I thought he might even smile, though he did not. '– Father Peter has disappeared.'

4

April 5, 1348

Will Fletcher thinks he is about to die.

The farm boys like Will sleep in the barns and the
Master has ordered they be given fresh straw to lie upon
once a month. But on account of his broken leg, Will was
brought in to the house. He can do no work, nor even walk
for all the splint Goodie Swift bound to his leg. So they
laid him out on a pallet of straw in a little room near the
kitchens that used to be a store once. I fancy it is colder
than the barn, but they put sacking over him for heat and

he does not have to listen to the other farm boys.

When the house is busy I get left alone more than when there is nothing much to do. I am little even for my age and since all believe me simple, I am given only simple tasks. ('Simple work for a simple girl,' says Goodie Swift.) Thus when people have much to do, they scarcely notice me so long as those simple tasks be done. So I scurry through the lower levels of the house like a mouse, keeping out of people's way, sometimes hiding to practise my writing, sometimes taking a little food as a mouse would, sometimes listening in on other people's conversations, which I know I should not, but I do anyway.

It was by listening that I learned the name of the new priest who frightened me on Sunday. He is called Father John, which is to say Father John Ellis. He is a stranger not alone to the village, but to the county and a friend of the Bishop, so they say. He is a man of much learning and holiness, and there is talk he may become personal chaplain to the Master, which Father Peter never was. But I do not care how important he is or how holy, for I do not like his eyes and I do not like it that he cuffed my ears on Sunday. Father Peter says it is almost a sin to punish someone on a Sunday, unless they were very, very wicked, which I was not.

For all my listening, I know no more of what has happened to Father Peter. I even asked Goodwife Swift, then later Goodwife Sharp, but neither had time for me and I think in any case they did not know.

I heard Will Fletcher groan as I passed by his room, and since the door was ajar I looked carefully to see and there was none with him. So I slipped inside, Jennet the mouse, to speak with him a moment. For Will has never teased me nor beaten me like the other farm boys, but always had a cheerful word and I liked him greatly.

He was all of a fever, his colour high and his eyes bright and wild. He stirred about on his pallet of straw and for a moment I thought he did not know me. But then he said, 'Jennet? Is that you, Jennet?'

'Aye, Will,' I said.

'My leg's sore, Jennet,' says he.

I could see it must be, for he had pushed away the sacking in his fever. The leg, with the breeches cut away, had swollen twice its own size or more. The black colour I had seen by the broken bone now ran well below his knee. His flesh oozed around the stick Mr Hacket had cut for a splint and the strips of cloth Goodie Swift had used to bind it. But the worst of it was the smell, like meat gone bad. 'It will be better soon,' I said to cheer him.

But Will said, 'Nay, Jennet, it will not be better soon or ever. They are sending for the barber.'

I felt mightily afraid then. When a limb is beyond saving, the barber cuts it away with a saw as a gardener might prune a rotten tree. If you are rich, which Will is not, they give you spirits of wine to drink. If you are poor, they give you a wad of leather to bite upon and tell the barber to work quickly. Afterwards, they burn the stump with hot irons to stop the bleeding, but even so most people die.

It seemed Will heard my thought, for he said in his hoarse fever-voice, 'I be about to die, Jennet. The barber will kill me.'

'You are strong, Will,' I told him, which was true enough. And even though he was near twenty, yet he was not so old. Most farm boys live past thirty, some past thirty-five.

'The barber will kill me,' Will repeated.

I crouched down beside him and took his hand, saying nothing. His eyes had grown moist and I cannot say for sure if he still knew I was there. So we stayed quiet, Will and me, and after a while he said, 'You're a good girl, Jennet. Will you pray for me?'

Father Peter taught me prayers for the sick, but whether

God listens to a servant girl I cannot say. All the same I nodded, for it would have been cruel to refuse him.

'Will you pray for me in the Master's chapel?' Will asked me, with the fire of fever bright in his eyes. 'God will hear you there.'

I was not allowed in the chapel unless I was sent by Goodwife Swift, but the worst of it would be a beating if I was caught and I had felt plenty of them. So I nodded again. 'I will pray for you in the chapel, Will,' I promised.

5

April 6, 1348

The barber will not come.

Goodie Swift is in such a fury that she broke a fine earthen pot and will be beaten for it if she cannot find someone else to blame. She calls the barber a lumpen weasel and much else besides. I have hidden from her these past two hours for she is in such a temper as would thrash me for nothing. All the same, I do not entirely blame her for she worries about poor Will Fletcher who now mutters and mumbles all his hours and knows no one except creatures in the corner that the rest of us cannot see.

While Will fears he will die if the barber cuts off his leg, Goodwife Swift fears he will die if the barber does not The limb is swollen huge and the stench so rank that even Will's close friends cannot stay with him. So however awful it be to lose a limb, Will cannot live with this one. It must be removed, says Goodie Swift, and buried in a pit of lime to halt the corruption. I think she is right, however fearful Will may be of it. I would tell Will so if he still knew me.

But the barber will not come and for a stupid reason. There is much talk in the village of a pestilence sent by God to punish sinners. The blue sickness, they call it and it has been brought to English shores by dirty foreign sailors and suchlike riff-raff. This is a plague like no other, for all who catch it die. They say their bodies swell and their faces turn black and neither prayer nor physic helps them. The sickness comes quick too, for they say some never even have time to show signs, but go to bed well and are dead by morning. It is a fearful thing.

This plague has come to London and towns in the south. These are port cities all, so you may believe it was carried in ships. But God is not mocked and the disease now travels by land, and those who know of it are sore afraid.

The barber knows of it, like all others of the village, but being a great fool he thinks it is the blue sickness that Will Fletcher has and not a broken leg. Goodie Swift sent word twice, and an angry word it was the second time, but still the barber will not believe it. Joan Fuller, who carried the message, says he took to crossing himself and wailing and chased her from his shop as if she were the Devil himself.

Now Goodie Swift threatens to take the case to the Master, for Will Fletcher is a hard worker and the Master would not want to lose him. If the Master says that the barber must come then come he will, for the anger of the Master is worse than any plague.

But I do not know if Goodie Swift will really take the case to the Master, for then he must find out about the pot she broke. And I do not know if the Master would send word to the barber in any case, for Will will do little work on the farm with only one leg and the Master may think it better to leave him die than feed a useless mouth.

The new priest, Father John, lodges at the house today although it is no longer Sunday and there is no requirement to say Mass. Goodwife Sharp asked him to pray over poor Will, but he told her he did not have time, on account of his many Godly works.

I wish Father Peter were here, for he would pray for Will and pray well. But still no one knows aught of Father Peter, whether he be alive or dead, nor where he went, nor what has happened to him. So if Will is to be prayed for, it will have to be me.

It will have to be soon as well. I scarce dare look in on Will for fear of what I might see. His poor leg is now wholly black. He raves and sweats and raves, then falls for short times into fitful sleep. But his eyes are never full closed, and if you look you can see the whites of them peeping out. He knows no one.

Will Fletcher is a strong man and I am a poor crippled scullery-maid who knows naught of anything, yet I know Death stalks him like a great black crow. If prayer or any other thing is to be of help, it must be soon. I could not get into the Master's chapel yesterday nor today for the new priest spends much time there and besides Goodwife Swift kept watchful eyes on me.

But I will go tonight, when the house sleeps. I will go then and I shall pray for Will.

6

April 6, 1348

This is the truth of it and I swear by God and his Holy Mother that I write no lie.

The Master is rich as any lord and near as rich as good King Edward himself, for each night there are torches and candles burning through the house so that the Master and his Lady might see where they walk. But not in the quarters of the servants, mind, for who would waste good tallow on the likes of us?

So when I crept from my straw, it was full dark as the

bowels of Satan and I had only my ears as a guide. I sleep with Becky and Ann and Joan and a dozen more, all of us scattered higgledy-piggledy on the straw bedding about the floor. There is no set place for any, but first come gets to keep away from draughts and burrow into fresh straw when there is any. I sought to lie by the door, on account of my mission, but Jane Burnham beat me to it and she be bigger than me so I could not chase her away.

So it was that when I rose, I had to pick my way to the door without treading on anyone and waking them up. I had no business to leave the sleeping chamber in the middle of the night and full well they knew it.

In the dark I had only my ears to guide me, but I listened for their breathing and trod gently, Jennet the mouse once more. I had in my mind where each was in relation to the others and this picture guided me as well, so that I reached the door having wakened none.

I was afraid the door might creak when I opened it

and so it did, but the grunts and the snores and the sleep breathing never faltered. So I slipped through and none knew I was gone. The corridor was cold besides dark, but I knew it well enough. Nor was it far to the chapel, and the approach was lit by torches in their sconces, tallow candles in their sticks. The chapel was in the main house, of course, not in the servants' quarters.

I should be beaten with a rod if someone found me here without good explanation. But there were none in the corridors and I hurried fast as my stupid foot would let me. Soon I reached the chapel which, being God's house, was never locked. I opened the door gently for fear someone might be inside, but when I looked, there was no one.

The chapel was candle-lit. They burn day and night in honour of God and His Holy Saints, so the place seems like Heaven itself with its fine drapes of red and purple and its statues and its great windows with their coloured glass. I went quickly to the altar and kneeled down as prettily as my twisted spine would allow. Then as Father Peter taught me, I clasped my hands and closed my eyes and made a prayer.

'Great and mighty God,' I prayed, 'Will Fletcher is sick and near to death. He needs the barber, but the barber will not come. Please God, send the barber and please let Will live when the barber cuts off his leg.'

Father Peter says the best prayer is when you ask God for exactly what it is you want without frills or fancies, and that seemed to be about it. But then I remembered how afraid Will was of the barber and added something more. 'Dear God,' I said, 'perchance You might cure Will without cutting his leg off since he is a good man who never teased me nor beat me.'

And that really did seem to be as much as I could say. I had done as I promised to Will, so I mumbled, 'Thank you, God' and struggled to get back on to my feet.

Behind me someone opened the chapel door.

7

April 6, 1348

Such fear. I know I have pretended it would be a beating if I were caught, but in truth I did not know what they would do to me. None but the Master and his Lady may enter the chapel without permission or just cause, and while I might enter to change the candles, getting caught now in the middle of the night might earn me a whipping or worse.

I ran at once to hide. In truth, if Goodie Swift had seen me she would not have believed it, for poor limping Jennet the mouse ran like the wind then, so frightened was she. I hid behind a hanging curtain and scarce dared breathe except to whisper another prayer to God to save me. Then I peered around the edge of the curtain and was even more afraid than I had been before, for it was Father John who had come in.

I near as sighed aloud, for he had not seen me. He was closing the door carefully as if to avoid making a sound. Then, when it was closed, he slid across the bar to lock it against any outside, as a priest does at the start of the Mass to prevent interruption. Was Father John about to say Mass now?

He did not walk in the chapel like a priest in his church. He moved slow, looking this way and that as if to make sure there was none but himself in the place. But he did not see me, Jennet the mouse, for I crouched down and stayed still and was hidden.

Yet if he did not see me, I saw him, for my hiding place let me see near the whole of the chapel. He walked to the high altar where I had prayed, and I thought for just a moment that he might pray too, but he did not. Nor did he stop by the altar, but moved beyond it to the cupboard where the Master keeps the silver and gold vessels for use in the Mass. I never heard Mass said in the chapel, but Father Peter once showed them to me and they are wonderful.

The cupboard is locked against thieves for the vessels are costly as well as holy, but Father John had a key. I saw him open the door and I saw him place the chalice and the platter and more besides into a little sack, much like the sack I use for the candles.

I was more afraid than ever then, for I am not so simple that I did not know this wicked priest was stealing from the Master. In my fear I knew I had to get away before he saw me. For if he saw me and knew I had seen him, it would not be a beating. He would never let me live!

In my mind I saw him murder me and bury my body in

the forest where none would find it. I am small and easily murdered, easily carried. And who would miss little Jennet the scullery maid? Not even Goodie Swift who would soon find someone else to scrub her pots.

Should I remain behind the curtain and wait for him to go? I was too frightened for that. Should I creep away while he was about his wicked work? I was too frightened for that, too. But the fear of staying was greater than the fear of going, so I slipped from my hiding place and tip-toed quiet as a mouse towards the door.

He did not hear me. He did not see me. I reached the door all of a stew, raised the latch and tugged, forgetting it was barred. My heart was bounding fit to leap from my breast. I slid the bar back quiet as I could and tried the latch again. The door opened. I was free!

'You, girl, what are you doing?' His voice filled the chapel like a great gong.

I ran. Oh how I ran.

8

April 7, 1348

I am to be tried for a witch.

Father John caught sight of me as I ran from the chapel. Worse, he knew me from the first time, so that he has told the Master I was there for thievery. Goodie Swift and Goodie Sharp and three strong farm boys came to take me where I lay burrowed, pretending sleep, with the others. So many come to take poor little Jennet the mouse.

They dragged me to the main house, to rooms and passages where I have never been, and took me to the Master.

So handsome he is close at hand, for I had never seen him before excepting at a distance. Such fine clothes, such bright polished boots. But his face was very stern.

Father John sat by him, drinking sack from the Master's goblet. I hate him now, that evil man. He serves Satan not God, and is a thief besides. But who would hear Jennet the mouse against a priest?

He told the Master I had crept into his chapel at dead of night, which was true. He said I had taken the consecrated host, Christ's holy body, for use in a spell. This I swear is not true. He said he thought I danced with Satan on the Saturday Sabbat and ran with the Wild Hunt and flew on a broomstick, none of which I could do.

I cried out in terror then, and said to the Master that Father John stole his chalice and his plate and put them in a sack. But the Master sent a serving man to the chapel to look, and the chalice and the plate were there as they had always been. A host was missing.

Father John required me then to confess and give up the sacred host so that it would be easier on me. But how could I confess what I did not do, and how could I give up what I did not have? They searched me, and when they did not find the host Father John said I must have hidden it, or eaten it, or ground it up in some vile potion.

They stripped me then, naked, in front of the Master and the priest and the menservants, and tied a blindfold round my eyes and pricked me. I called out with the pain, pleading with them to stop, but one time they pricked me so light I did not feel it and did not cry out. Father John said that was the Devil's mark on me, which can give no pain.

They searched the place where I slept and there found Bright Eyes. A stable boy caught him easily enough and brought him to the Master. Father John said this was my familiar, an evil spirit in animal form, proof positive I was in league with Satan. They took Bright Eyes away then, and though I begged and pleaded I thought they must kill him.

'What's to be done?' asked the Master then. 'She's no more than a child.'

'A wicked child,' Father John told him. 'Old enough to do the work of Satan. She must be punished. It is a matter of spiritual evil.'

The Master did not seem convinced. 'What do I know of spiritual evil? Shall we cane her? Shall we flog her? What?'

'She must be put to death,' said Father John.

9

April 8, 1348

Will Fletcher died in the night. Becky whispered the news
through the door of my cell, even though none was supposed to talk to me. His was not the only death. Becky
whispered that the blue sickness has come to Potter's Field,
which is not our village, but a village near. There is great
panic. Many are ill and three have already died. Becky
said that the Bishop who is to try me preached that this
was God's judgement for heresy and witchery and sin.
When she told me, I feared I was judged already.

They took me to the Great Hall where the Master sat with the Bishop and my accuser, Father John, along with three other clerics. I did not know these three at all. They were young men who attended the Bishop. The Bishop was a tall man, taller than the Master, all dressed in purple with a face like a death's head. But his voice was kindly enough, which surprised me, for I had heard Father John was his friend and so supposed he would be against me.

He told me I should fear nothing were I a good girl and a good Christian, but only fear if the charges against me were true. He said I stood accused of heresy and witchery and truck with the Devil, as well as theft of the Holy Body of Our Lord. He said the Church had power to try me, but that I should be passed to the civil court for sentence were I found guilty. He asked me if I understood and I said I did, though I did not.

One of the young clerics made a great speech then, calling the Court to order and naming the Bishop as judge and me, Jennet Farr, as the accused. And after that, it was Father John who stood and filled the air with his wicked, wicked lies.

I knew I was doomed. His colour was high and he was sweating greatly, but he spoke with such force that all must believe him. He sneezed once, near the start, but otherwise did not pause so much as a moment in his lies. He told of seeing me in the chapel and seeing me steal the host. He swore I must have fed it to my familiar, and one of the young clerics brought forth Bright Eyes in a box. He looked frightened and my heart went out to him, but at least he was alive.

Father John told how I had been pricked and felt no pain, and said my hare lip was another Devil's mark, my twisted spine a punishment from God for my wickedness. He grew excited then and spittle flew from his mouth. His eyes were wild and angry, and I thought of Will's eyes at the height of his fever. He waved his arms and pointed and shouted, so that even the Bishop seemed uneasy. Then at the end of it, he fell to the floor in a fit.

Two of the young clerics ran forward to attend to him, but stopped.

'It is the blue sickness,' said one, his voice no louder than a whisper.

Father John jerked and turned his head, and black bile oozed from his mouth. His eyes were open but I thought he saw no one.

'The blue sickness?' asked the Bishop. He stood up with such haste that his chair fell over.

Father John began to shiver then, like one who has grown cold. He moaned like a lost soul who has seen the gates of hell.

'He has the blue sickness!' said the Master, his eyes wide.

'He has the blue sickness!' someone else screamed, I know not who.

And of a sudden they were all running from the Great Hall, the Bishop and the Master, and the clerics and the men who guarded me, and the others beside who had come to see me tried. They pushed and shoved at one another in their haste. They stumbled and caught themselves, and elbowed and jostled and used unseemly words.

I was alone with Father John. But Father John could do me no more harm. He threshed upon the floor and tore his clothes, and I saw an unsightly swelling that had come underneath his arm. 'Help me,' he said. 'Help me, child.' But I stayed well distant from him.

Since there was none left to stop me, I picked up Bright Eyes in his box and hurried from the Great Hall. Then, because I met none in the passages, I hurried from the house.

10

April 12, 1348

I hid three days and three nights in the forest. Bright Eyes stayed with me close on two days, but left to fend for himself when I could not feed him. I knew I should not see him again, but I was pleased he had returned to his wild home at last. I found berries to eat, but not many, and on the fourth day hunger and the sound of wolves forced me to leave the forest.

I took the road to the village, for I knew no other place to go. I thought to find some food there, then press on. It was not safe to stay in the village for the Master and his men rode there often, and if I was discovered I would surely be taken back to face the Bishop.

It was no easy walk, for I was weak with hunger and my back pained me greatly from sleeping in a poor position. Worse, it had rained in the night and was raining now and the road was muddy. But at last I saw the church spire on the horizon, and knew I had not far to go. It was then that I met with a man and a woman who looked as weary and as frightened as I did.

The woman carried a baby wrapped in rags against the cold. The man was harnessed like a horse to the shafts of a small cart. The cart carried a few pots and pans and some bundles of the things they owned.

'Turn back, child,' the woman called. 'You will die if you go on.'

'It's the blue sickness,' said the man. 'God's anger is upon us.'

They did not stop, not for a moment, but moved past me, their eyes fixed on the road ahead. The baby in the rags coughed once and whined then was quiet. Nor did I stop, despite this warning, for if I did not go to the village, where else should I go? Better the risk of the blue sickness than the certainty of death by hunger. I placed my eye on the steeple, prayed silently for God's mercy and trudged on through the mud and the rain.

I saw the first of the houses and a body on the road outside. She was a woman in a rough brown kirtle lying curled up like an infant. I know not if she was dead, for I feared to approach. There were other bodies soon, some living, some dead, left where they fell. I thought to enter one of the cottages to search for food for who would stop me? But I liked not the idea of stealing, hungry though I was. So I walked on, trusting in God's mercy and hoping to find one at least who would take pity on me.

The village stank of death. In truth I saw more dead

than living and many who were not dead but soon would be. The blue sickness is a fearsome thing. Small wonder the Master and the Bishop had fled from it. If Father John truly had it, I pitied him. I saw many who were far gone in their illness. Their faces were blue-black, their bodies swollen, their skin cracked. Some vomited without pause. Others lay staring upwards at the sky, not even blinking when the raindrops fell into their eyes. They moaned and muttered and cursed and prayed, and called to friends who were not there. I thought I walked in hell.

Yet if I did, there were angels there. In the market square I saw good men who tried to clear away the dead, lifting the corpses on to carts and drawing them off for decent burial. And I saw good men and women both who sought to aid the sick. One saw me and said, 'Do you have the sickness, child?'

I shook my head and said only, 'Hungry.' She gave me bread to eat and cheese.

The food revived me greatly and I determined to move on, part in fear of the Master and the Bishop, part in the hope of finding a place the blue sickness had not visited. Thus I sought the road onwards, but as I left the village a voice called my name.

11

April 12, 1348

My dragging foot betrayed me. I ran and ran. So fast I ran,

knowing that the Master or the Bishop had discovered me,

but then my foot caught on a root or stone or I know not

what, and I fell face down in the mud. Next thing hands

were upon me, strong hands I could not escape. I knew I

was taken and would be tried again and judged a witch and

hanged.

But the hands helped me up and wiped mud from my

face and eyes. I twisted to break free, but the man who

held me said, 'Easy, Jennet, easy!' as if talking to a nervous horse.

Then I looked into his dear sweet face. 'Father Peter!' I cried out and hugged him and held him and wept and wept as if my heart must break.

'There, child,' he whispered, holding me and patting my back. 'There, child, you are safe.'

'I thought you were dead!' I wailed. So I had, though I told no one.

'Near as dead,' he said. 'I had the blue sickness, but God spared me.'

I clung to him so tightly then. 'Father Peter!' I said. 'Father Peter!' It was all I could say.

In a while he gently eased me away from him and held me distant by my shoulders. In truth he still looked tired and ill. His skin clung to his bones without flesh beneath and his eyes were dark and sunken. His parson's cloth hung as if there was no more than a skeleton beneath. But there was no swelling, no stench of decay. The sickness had taken him and wrung him dry, then left him.

'The plague has taken the village,' Father Peter said. 'Many have died of it. Good people, too. I do not understand why God punishes those who have led decent lives yet leaves sinners untouched. And yet He strikes down sinners too. Some live, some die, some are untouched by the sickness entirely. Are you ill, Jennet? You look thin.'

'I am not ill, Father,' I said. Then all of a rush, 'They think I am a witch!' and I told him what had passed at the Great House and how Father John had accused me.

He listened without a word, then said, 'You need have no fear, Jennet. Father John is dead. God saw his sins and punished him. Your Master and his Lady and the Bishop have all fled the county for fear of the plague, as if God could not seek them out if He wished. But they will not trouble you now. No one cares what Father John said you did. They all seek to save themselves from the sickness.'

I knew not what to do then. I had thought only of running and hiding, and now I had no need of either. All my life I lived in the Great House. My mother was a servant there who died giving birth to me. It was her punishment, Goodie Swift said. I was raised an orphan by the Master's charity and put to work as soon as I could walk. But I could not go back there now. The Master may have fled, but if God spared him he would return. I looked at Father Peter. 'I have nowhere to go.'

'Then you must stay here and help me tend to those in need,' Father Peter said. 'Do you fear the blue sickness?'

In truth I did not. For God spares who He chooses and hunts down those who would flee His wrath. He had spared me in my hour of danger and struck down the wicked priest who sought my death. I did not think He would visit the blue sickness on me now.

I smiled at Father Peter. 'I will stay with you,' I said.

Life in

Medieval

England

The Black Death

The year 1333 opened badly in China. Drought in earlier years led to crop failure and famine. Everybody prayed for rain and in 1333 their prayers were answered . . . with a flood that swept across the central plains and drowned 400,000 people. The flooding was so great an entire mountain collapsed, leaving a gaping hole to show where it once stood.

Just twelve months later the drought came back. Locusts then ate up the last of the crops and there was famine again. Volcanoes erupted. For nearly ten years, earthquake followed flood followed earthquake. Even for a country as used to disasters as China, it must have seemed like the end of the world.

But worse was to come.

In nearby Central Asia, people began to die in their thousands from a mysterious disease. It spread eastwards into China. There were 5,000,000 victims in one province alone.

China is a huge country and in the fourteenth century the fastest form of transport for most people was the bullock-cart, so the plague was slow to spread outside. But eventually it began to cross borders. The results were terrifying. By 1346 many countries of Asia and the Middle East had gone down with the disease. India lost much of its huge population. Tartary, Mesopotamia, Syria, Armenia were covered with dead bodies. The Kurds fled in vain to their mountains.

The vicious nature of the disease was mind-bending. First signs appeared suddenly. In a few hours your temperature rose to about 40°C (104°F). You became horribly ill, vomiting without pause. You had cramps and muscle pain. Your mind began to wander, so you could not think clearly. After a while, you fell into a raving dream.

Lymph nodes are little glands in your body that help you fight off disease. There are clusters of them in your neck, groin and armpits. But once this disease struck, instead of fighting it off, your lymph nodes just swelled up and filled with pus. Nine times out of ten, you were dead within days. Sometimes within hours. Accounts written at the time tell how people went to bed healthy and were found as putrid corpses the next morning.

Word of the plague spread ahead of the plague itself, but got exaggerated. One writer claimed the disaster had begun with a rain of frogs. This was followed by a day-long hail storm during which sheets of fire wiped out the population of 'a certain province, hard by Greater India'. On the third day more fire from heaven finished off the job in a cloud of stinking smoke.

It was the cloud that caught people's imagination. In those days, nobody knew what caused disease so many concluded that the plague came from the air going bad like rotting meat. The same writer had the idea that . . .

. . . through the foul blast of wind that comes

from the South, the whole seashore and sur-

rounding lands were infected.

Another told of a great rain of fire between Cathay (China) and Persia (Iran), then went on to say:

And there arose vast masses of smoke; and whosoever beheld this died within the space of half a day; and likewise any man or woman who looked upon those who had seen this.

The disease began to crawl down the silk roads into Europe. Those routes from the Far East that had for centuries brought silk, spices and other goods to the West, now brought death. The plague moved from Baghdad along the Tigris through Armenia. By 1346, it reached the Italian trade stations in the Crimea. Within months, the death toll climbed to 85,000. Local Tartars decided it was all the fault of Christian merchants and attacked a Genoese trading station in the city of Tana. The merchants fled to Feodosia on the coast. Pursuing Tartars settled down outside the city walls to lay siege. But before they could do much, the plague had caught up with them. In days they were dying like flies.

The Tartars decided to call off the siege, but not before giving the Christians a taste of their own medicine. They had noticed that anybody who came close to plague victims often fell ill themselves, so they loaded the pus-filled bodies into giant catapults and flung them over the city walls.

The Genoese dumped the corpses into the sea, but the damage was already done. We now know that bubonic plague is caused by bacteria. This bacteria (which is called *Yersinia pestis*) is usually carried by fleas that have fed on infected rats. After a flea has taken in blood, the plague bacteria multiply in its stomach and eventually block it altogether. Then, when the flea feeds again, the obstruction causes the blood to be vomited back into the bite, along with plague bacteria. In carrying the Tartar corpses through their town to the sea, the Genoese just gave the fleas new people to bite. Within days the whole city was infected.

As plague killed thousands in Feodosia, its citizens quickly realised the few left could never defend against another Tartar attack. There was a panic-stricken retreat by sea. Plague-ridden rats and fleas climbed into the ships along with the fearful Genoese.

These ships, along with trading galleys from infected Eastern ports, put in at Genoa, at Venice, at Messina, but by then their crews were dying at the oars. When the port authorities saw the cargoes of corpses, they sent the ships packing. But action always came a little too late. While the authorities made their inspections, fleas hopped, rats scuttled ashore and the plague landed. Banished from their docks, the galleys simply sought other ports, thus spreading the disease even further. By 1347, the plague – now known as the 'blue sickness' – was raging throughout Sicily. Three months later, it had taken a firm hold on Italy.

Towards the end of January 1348, the dreadful pattern repeated. A plague-ridden galley, banished from Italy, put in at Marseilles, in France. Port authorities came on board to inspect and left infected. The ship was chased off and carried its cargo of death to Spain.

By 1350, *Yersinia pestis* had continued its dreadful progress eastwards into Germany. It seems to have reached Bavaria first, then travelled north along the Moselle Valley. By this time it was already well established in Cyprus, in Greece and in Turkey. Watching its progress in Constantinople, an historian wrote:

> *The calamity did not destroy men only, but*
> *many animals living with and domesticated*
> *by men. I speak of dogs and horses, and all*

the species of birds, even the rats that hap-

pened to live within the walls of houses.

Dalmatia was plague-ridden. Dubrovnik went under in the opening weeks of 1348. When the plague reached the town of Split two months later, wolves poured in from the neighbouring forests to attack the few survivors. Piles of corpses rotted in the streets – there was no one left to bury them.

The horror reached England at about the same time. Nobody is quite sure where the plague struck first. It may have been Bristol or Southampton both of which traded a lot with the continent, but experts think Melcombe Regis (now part of Weymouth) was the most likely place. Medical archives describe how two ships docked at this Dorset port a few days before the Feast of St John the Baptist in 1348. A sailor on one of them was already suffering from the illness, picked up in Gascony.

He infected the town. Soon the plague spread throughout the entire country.

Having accepted the nightmare gift from Europe, England sent it on to Scandinavia. The crew of a wool ship that sailed from London in 1349 succumbed to the plague while at sea and died to a man. The vessel eventually ran aground near Bergen in Norway. Looters carried away more than they bargained from the wreck.

The blue sickness spread south into Denmark and east into Sweden. King Magnus II saw it coming. In 1350 he announced to his subjects that the 'great punishment of God' had killed off most of the Norwegians, that pestilence was raging in the Netherlands and that if the Swedes did not mend their ways, they would soon be in the same boat. Penances were introduced, including fasting and barefoot processions around churchyards, but the plague came just the same. The King survived. Two of his brothers died.

The pestilence now raging in the European heartland killed 75,000,000 people before burning itself out. This was between a quarter and a half of the total population of the continent.

It was not the first time the plague had struck – it had killed an estimated 100,000,000 people in the Middle East, Europe, and Asia during the sixth century, and some people blame it for the fall of the Roman Empire.

Outbreaks of the Black Death, as historians now call it, continued to ravage the world for the next 200 years. The Great Plague of London raged from 1664 through 1665 until the Great Fire of London put a stop to it in 1666. It resulted in more than 70,000 deaths in a population of 460,000. An outbreak in Canton and Hong Kong in 1894 left 80,000 to 100,000 dead. Within 20 years the disease spread, resulting in more than 10,000,000 deaths world-wide. In recent times, smaller epidemics have occurred in Southeast Asia, India, Africa and South America. Even in a country like the United States, scattered cases were reported as late as 1968.

Of all the illnesses humanity has faced, *Yersinia pestis* is undoubtedly the most persistent, the most horrifying and the most difficult to treat. It comes in three forms: bubonic, pneumonic and septicaemic. The ghastly outbreak in the fourteenth century contained all three. Bubonic plague, spread by rats and fleas, was marked by lymph gland swellings. Pneumonic plague, which attacked the victim's lungs, spread far more quickly since it was carried on the breath. Septicaemic plague, which attacked the blood, was the most deadly. This was the one that killed people overnight.

Even today, doctors cannot afford to take plague lightly. Death almost always comes if you aren't given the right antibiotics – introduced in 1941 – within *15 hours* of your first symptoms. In the Middle Ages, doctors working without antibiotics were powerless to halt the advance of the disease. Although they developed many treatments, none worked.

People started to take their own precautions. Anyone forced to go outside carried 'smelling-apples' (balls of camphor, pepper, sandalwood and other ingredients) or bunches of flowers. Any time you hear the nursery rhyme 'Ring-a-Roses', you are listening to a description of plague times. The 'ring-a-roses' referred to the reddish purple swellings on the skin. The 'pocketful of posies' were the flowers people carried to try to protect themselves. 'Atissue!' was the first sneeze that showed you'd got the illness. 'We all fall down' was what happened very quickly afterwards.

Most doctors agreed with the priests that plague was a punishment from God, caused by the spread of gambling, or the misbehaviour of women, or any one of a hundred other supposed sins. They argued among themselves about whether figs or lettuce or aubergines might be used as cures. They talked about invisible streams that flowed through the nostrils into the brain and destroyed the memory. They made poultices from excrement. They let blood from weakened patients. They purged with the 'perpetual pill', a pellet of metallic antimony that was fished from the chamber pot when it had done its job and wiped down before being stored for future use. They wore multi-coloured shirts stained with magical chalks to protect against the disease.

All around them, thousands died.

The Church

On October 31, 1517, Martin Luther posted his Ninety-five Theses on the door of the Castle Church, Wittenberg and laid the foundations of Protestantism. But in Jennet's day, 'the Church' meant the Roman Catholic Church. It was a far cry from the respected institution it is today.

Over the centuries, the Church had involved itself

deeply in European politics. This meant intrigue, backbiting, manipulation and dirty tricks. While all these things brought increased power and wealth, they tended to cast questions on the Church's spiritual authority.

But the Pope walked in arrogance, ignoring all criticism. The Church became a sort of supernatural protection racket, selling indulgences (which meant you were let off any sin) and spiritual privileges (which meant you were allowed to sin again for free).

Another popular item of trade was holy relics. If you glued together all the pieces of the 'True Cross' offered for sale in Europe at the time, you would have enough wood to build a ship. Dead saints miraculously produced more bones than the human body contains, sometimes even several heads. Their mummified hands were supposed to protect from all sorts of misfortunes. Superstition was actively encouraged – it was good for business. When illness struck, the priest was often called before the doctor.

And not to administer Last Rites, but to cure.

(The priest was not the only one believed – against all evidence – to have natural healing powers. The disease scrofula, a swelling of the lymph glands, was known as the 'King's Evil' because it could, so people thought, be cured by a single touch from the monarch. Three hundred years after Jennet's time, Charles II administered to 90,000 sufferers during his reign.)

Like the modern Mafia it so much resembled, the medieval Church was jealous of its power. In an age when Satan was believed to walk the Earth each night, there was no room for anybody who challenged Church authority. Nowhere was this more visible than in the persecution of witches.

In 1231, Pope Gregory IX set up the Inquisition, a special church body dedicated to tracking down heretics and bringing them to trial. Twenty-one years later, another Pope, Innocent IV, ruled that torture could be used in this holy work. The definition of heresy included the practice of witchcraft.

Witchcraft itself is something of a puzzle. Some authorities believe it was a relic of the old pagan religions practised in Ancient Greece and Rome. Others give it deeper roots, dating back to the widespread Goddess-worship of prehistory. Still others think it never really existed outside the fevered imaginations of Churchmen who disliked women at the best of times and grabbed any stick to beat them.

Whatever the reality of witchcraft itself, the *belief* in witchcraft was certainly real and that was enough to begin one of the most vicious persecutions the world has ever known. An accusation of witchcraft was enough to get a woman jailed, stripped and searched for the 'Devil's Mark' – any skin blemish or eruption that could be interpreted as being placed by Satan. She might then be tested by pricking with needles until a spot on her body was discovered where she felt no pain. Alternatively, she might be thrown into the nearest lake. If she floated, it was believed that the water had rejected her because she was a witch. If she sank and drowned, she was judged innocent.

Any witch who survived initial testing was held in isolation and encouraged to confess by a little judicious torture. This varied from the application of burning brimstone (sulphur) to the more sensitive parts of the body, to the breaking of limbs and the crushing of bones. When toes were amputated the witch was often given a small bag of her own bones as a souvenir of the experience. If she died under torture or was subsequently convicted, her family was sent a bill for the cost of the materials used to kill her.

Convicted witches were hanged or burned alive. If they confessed their sins, they were sometimes accorded the 'mercy' of being strangled beforehand.

Nobody, but nobody, wanted to be accused of witchcraft.

Lifestyle

Food was no fun in the fourteenth century.

If you were poor, you couldn't get enough of it – and what you did get was repetitive and tasteless. If you were rich, you ate yourself into an early grave on huge quarters of beef, mutton, wild boar, hedgehog and even peacock cooked on spits or in smoke-black cauldrons near the tables. Everything was seasoned with so much ginger, cinnamon, cloves, and nutmeg that you couldn't taste the meat. Which was just as well since a lot of it was bad.

Nothing else was much fun either. Life was frankly bleak. Most people died of old age in their thirties, stricken by poor nourishment and abysmal sanitation. You drew your water from a well and carried it into the house in pails. You seldom washed and never bathed. Unless you were very very rich indeed, your lavatory was a heavily-stained chamber pot or a convenient bush. Toilet paper was unheard of. Your clothes were itchy, flea-infested, rough and dull. It was the middle of the century before the crocus was introduced into a small Essex settlement that had grown up around a Norman Abbey. That allowed the manufacture for the first time of yellow dye and gave the settlement the name it carries to this day – Saffron Walden.

Jennet was lucky to work in a great house. Although she was not paid much – and may not have been paid at all – she was at least fed and sheltered. Those who worked the land were often faced with starvation or eviction in the wake of a poor harvest or a greedy landlord (who took a portion of their crop as rent).

Society was divided into four broad sections: the aristocracy, the professional religious, the military and the rest. Those few in the first three categories had some degree of power over their lives. The rest had none. But even for the richest noble or bishop, life was not particularly pleasant. It couldn't be. The comforts we take for granted today simply didn't exist.

In the fouteenth century, you rose with the sun and went to bed when it grew dark. Only the wealthy could afford candles and even they tended to use them sparingly. Since glass was rare, windows tended to be small, so rooms were dark and frequently both damp and cold. When you lit a fire, your habitation tended to fill with smoke. There was no electricity, of course, no running water, no sanitation, no flush toilets, no central heating, no radio, no television. For entertainment there was story-telling by the fire and, for the rich, the occasional visit of a minstrel troupe. But in all honesty there was little need for entertainment. People were usually far too tired to appreciate it.

Life was, in the main, both stagnant and colourless.

Stagnant because the fine old Roman roads had long since fallen into disrepair, so that while people still moved about, they moved only a short distance. The vast majority walked. The wealthy used a saddle horse or wagon. But good wagons were hard to find, so that this uncomfortable means of transport was eventually reserved for the truly desperate – the sick.

Colourless because the fine dyes and paints taken for granted today did not exist. The predomonant colours were the green of grass, the brown of mud and the black of smoke. Only in the stained glass of the churches did the common people experience a broader spectrum.

They must have felt they were being granted a fore-taste of heaven.

Disease

The Black Death was not the only disease Jennet and her companions had to deal with. They faced epidemics of leprosy, smallpox, tuberculosis, scabies, anthrax, trachoma and sweating sickness. But the real peculiarity was some-thing now called dancing mania.

Anyone infected by dancing mania was driven to dance

until they fell down exhausted – in some cases fell down dead. The earliest manifestations of the disease were in Spain, where it was believed to be caused by the bite of the tarantula spider (thus naming the popular Tarantella dance). Epidemics of the illness spread throughout Europe for a time, then stopped. Today, doctors have no idea what caused the outbreak, except that it was definitely *not* a spider bite.

Leprosy was widespread in Jennet's day, and the only way to deal with it was to isolate those who caught it. Leper colonies were formed where those with the disease watched their extremities slowly rot as they waited for death. At first, there was some attempt to treat the Black Death the same way.

Jennet's story is set in 1348, the year the Black Death arrived in England. But the epidemic itself raged for three full years. In the early days, anyone who caught it was held in isolation for 14 days on the theory that by then they would either have recovered or died. But as the disease continued to spread, the isolation period gradually increased to 40 days.

The plague had an upside. It eventually forced the authorities to look for pure water supplies, install observation stations, build isolation hospitals and improve garbage disposal and food safety. But before this happened, in Jennet's own time, your chances of recovery from illness were generally slim.

A large part of the problem was the general state of medicine. The very best medical training harked back to the ideas – often simply wrong – of ancient Roman physicians like Galen. The first thing a good doctor learned was astrology, since it was believed that the positions of the planets influenced both the course of a disease and its cure. Medication was frequently prescribed on the basis of a patient's horoscope rather than his symptoms.

The theory of 'humours' was popular. This classified

diseases in relation to a small number of mysterious currents believed to flow through the body. When a humour got out of balance you became sick. Nobody knew about viruses or bacteria. Infectious disease was sometimes believed to be the result of foul air. Nobody knew about the circulation of the blood, although leeches were often used to draw out fever.

Surgery, as we understand it today, was unknown too. No operation existed that could help Jennet's hare lip or twisted spine. The nearest thing to a surgeon was the local barber, who combined haircuts and shaves with the occasional amputation.

Will may have been lucky the barber refused to call on him. Had the barber done so, he would have faced the removal of his leg without anaesthetic. Patients remained conscious, held or tied down in searing agony as the barber cut through flesh and sawed through bone, then cauterised the stump afterwards with fire.

A really good barber/surgeon was judged by just one thing – how fast he could work. Most patients died. Payment for services was extracted in advance.

The Progress of the Plague

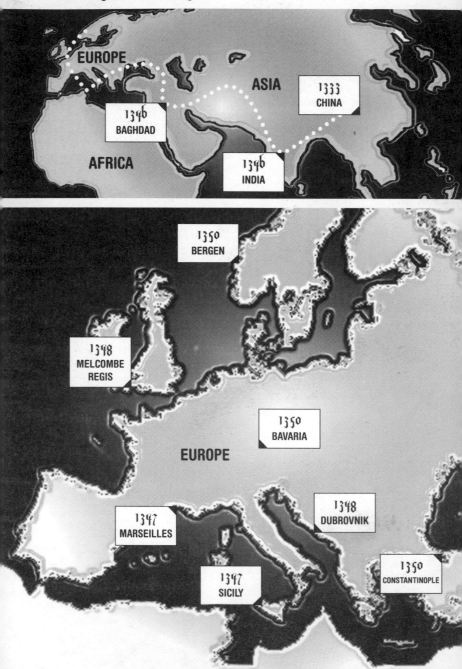